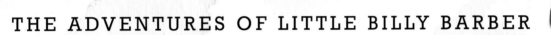

THE ADVENTURES OF LITTLE BILLY BARBER

Billy's First Flight Lesson

Written by Elaine R. Barber • Illustrated by Linda Terentiak

AMP&RSAND, INC.

Chicago • New Orleans

ISBN 978-145070620-9

Designed by
David Robson
Robson Design

Published by
AMPERSAND, INC.
1050 North State Street
Chicago, Illinois 60610

203 Finland Place
New Orleans, Louisiana 70131

www.ampersandworks.com

Printed in Canada

In loving memory of Captain William A. Barber,
who always said, "I can't believe how lucky I am.
I'm actually getting paid for something I would
gladly do for free!" Truly a blessed man.

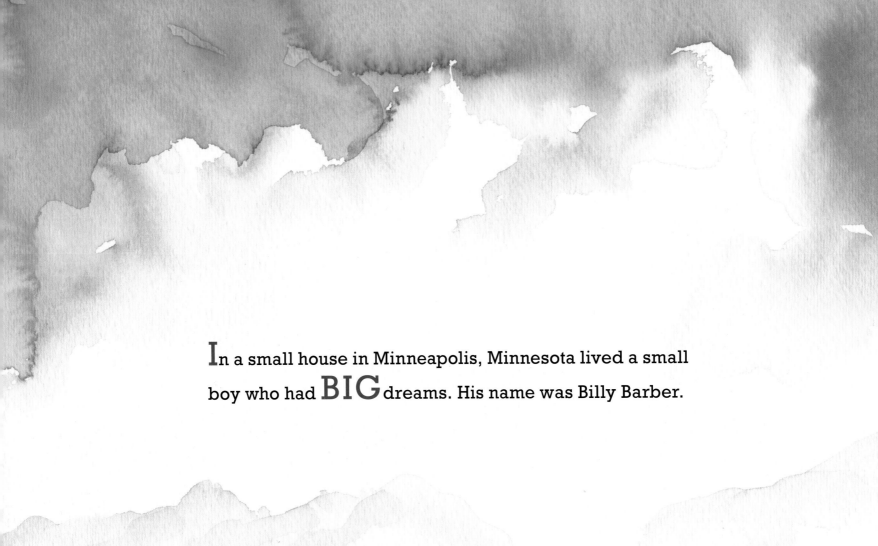

In a small house in Minneapolis, Minnesota lived a small boy who had **BIG** dreams. His name was Billy Barber.

LOCKHEED ORION MODEL 10

DOUGLAS DC-3 AIRLINER

Billy dreamt of flying. At breakfast, he made runways in his oatmeal and flew his spoon around his bowl. Sometimes he stretched out his arms and flew around the kitchen. Scooping up his books, he'd swoop down and kiss his mother good-bye and then fly out the front door.

Z O O O O M !

Every day after school, Billy rode his bike to the Minneapolis Airport. He spent hours watching airplanes take off and land. Airplanes of every shape and size were stored in the big white hangar.

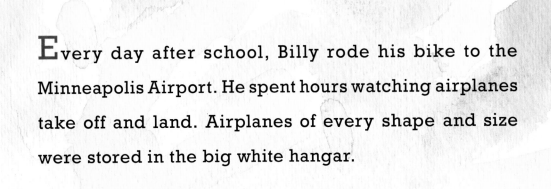

PAN AMERICAN "CHINA CLIPPER" FLYING BOAT

LOCKHEED ELECTRA

One day, Billy wanted to get a closer look. He hid his bike in the tall grass, jumped over the fence, walked into the hangar and tip-toed around the planes. Some had two wings, some had four, some had high wings, and some were low.

"Hey kid, how did you get in here?"

The pilot startled him. "I just wanted to see the airplanes up close," gulped Billy.

"What's your name, kid?"

"Billy—I mean Bill, Bill Barber." Billy tried to sound older.

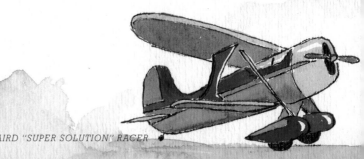

LAIRD "SUPER SOLUTION" RACER

FORD TRI-MOTOR

"You're the kid who's always hanging out at the fence. You like airplanes, I bet."

"One day, I'm going to fly and be a great pilot," Billy said.

"Have you ever been in a plane?" the pilot asked.

"Last summer. An air show troop came to town and the pilot of a Ford Tri-Motor asked me to sell tickets for plane rides. At the end of the day he took me up," Billy said. He was b u r s t i n g with pride.

STEARMAN

"How would you like some first class help around here?" Billy asked.

"Are you saying you want a job? I guess I could use some help around here. How about a trade? I will pay for your time in flight lessons."

"Flight lessons?! Hot dog!"

"At the end of each month, I'll take you up for a 30 minute flight lesson."

"Sir, you've got yourself a deal!" Billy said holding out his hand.

When Billy got home, he opened the front door, put out his arms as wide as he could, revved up his engine and flew down the hall, into the living room, into the kitchen and around his mother.

"**Please**, please, please, Mom! Please don't say no! You just **have** to say **yes**!

"Mom! A pilot at the airport gave me a job today. He said he would trade me flight lessons for work! I can ride my bike there after school. Is it ok? Can I? Please?!"

"Well, all right, but you'd better keep up with your homework and..."

Billy was so happy, he flew down the hall and landed in his room.

1930s ERA HANGARS

WACO CABIN BIPLANE

Every day after school, Billy worked hard. He helped to push planes around, handed the pilot tools, swept the hangar floor, washed airplanes and ran to the front office for coffee. Whenever he had a spare moment Billy would sit in the cockpit of one of the airplanes and pretend he was flying up, up into the big blue sky, doing rolls, spins and loops.

At last it was time for Billy's first flight lesson. He was so excited! He scrambled out of bed, threw on his clothes and was running out the front door when his mother called, "Billy, come and eat. You need something in your stomach on this very important day!

"No runways in your oatmeal this morning?"

"Mom, that's kid's stuff! Today I leave a boy and come back a pilot!"

O.X. TRAVELAIR 2000

GEE BEE

When Billy got to the hangar, the pilot walked over to him. "Look kid, I'm sorry but I can't take you up today. We're having a problem. The Gee Bee's right rudder pedal is stuck."

Billy could not believe his ears. This was supposed to be his ADVENTURE DAY!

"I'll help you fix it!" Billy grabbed a wrench and nudged his way through for a peek inside.

"If I can fix the plane, will you take me up for my first flight lesson right now?"

"Sure kid, but what makes you think you can fix it?"

"I think I see the problem."

Billy climbed into the cockpit, squeezed his small hand under the rudder pedal and pulled out a little black button. He gave the rudder a push and POP! The pedal eased UP.

STINSON

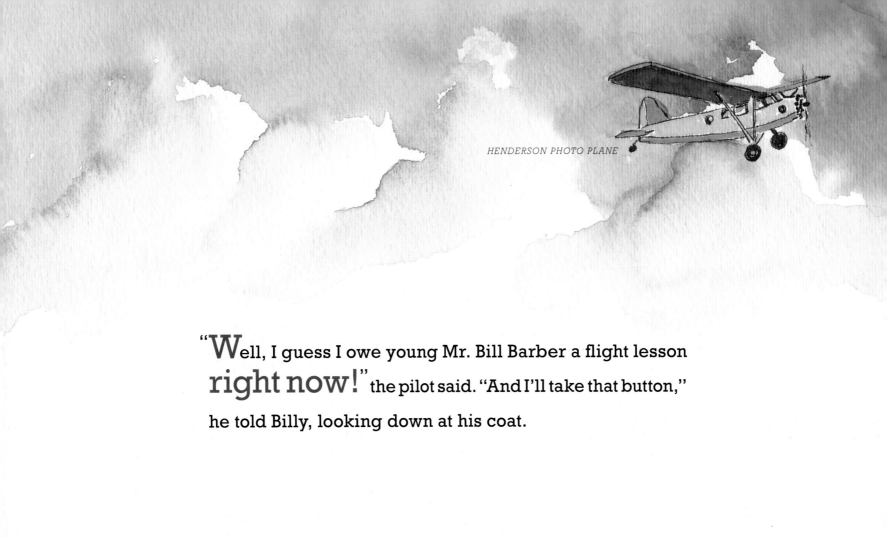

HENDERSON PHOTO PLANE

"**W**ell, I guess I owe young Mr. Bill Barber a flight lesson **right now!**" the pilot said. "And I'll take that button,"

he told Billy, looking down at his coat.

Billy and the pilot walked towards the Piper Cub, a small yellow airplane with a long black lightning bolt painted on each side. The flight lesson began with a pre-flight inspection.

PIPER J3 CUB

PIPER J3 CUB

The pilot buckled Billy into the seat and taxied down the runway, going faster and faster until the plane left the ground. Billy saw the pilot motion for him to take the control stick. Nervous, but filled with excitement, he grabbed the stick.

"I'm flying! I'm really flying!"

Billy flew over the runway, over the town and over his own little house. Z O O O O M !

William A. Barber
(1925–1987)

CAPTAIN WILLIAM A. BARBER

was destined to become a world-class pilot. He first soloed at the age of 11 in his native Minnesota. In his mid-20s, Bill became one of the youngest commercial airline captains in the United States. He logged more than 30,000 hours of pilot and command time. In 1962, he was Captain of the first United States Aerobatic Team which competed in Budapest, Hungry. Barber was a flying renaissance man whose aerobatic career spanned more than 25 years. He performed crowd pleasing air show acts that included dead-stick sequences, rope-ladder pickup, car-top landing, team aerobatics, sky writing, wing-walking and comedy shows. He was awarded the Wilkinson Sword of Excellence and was inducted into the International Aerobatic Hall of Fame, the Minnesota Aviation Hall of Fame and the Michigan Aviation Hall of Fame.

Each year at the AirVenture Show in Oshkosh, Wisconsin, this award is given to an airshow performer extraordinaire who has demonstrated superb showmanship ability.

BILL BARBER AWARD FOR SHOWMANSHIP
FOR DEMONSTRATING SUPERB AIRSHOW SHOWMANSHIP!
Sponsored by *World Airshow News* (www.airshowmag.com)
and Family and Friends of Bill Barber
(especially Bob Barden)

The Winners

2010	Steve Oliver and Suzanne Asbury-Oliver	**1998**	Patty Wagstaff
2009	Mike Goulian	**1997**	Gene Soucy and Teresa Stokes
2008	Bud Granley	**1996**	Wayne Handley
2007	Dacy Family Airshow Team	**1995**	Bob Hoover
2006	Danny Clisham	**1994**	Bob and Annette Hosking (Otto)
2005	Kent and Warren Pietsch	**1993**	Red Baron Stearman Squadron
2004	Bobby Younkin	**1992**	Sean D. Tucker
2003	Jim LeRoy	**1991**	Julie Clark
2002	AeroShell Aerobatic Team	**1990**	Leo Loudenslager
2001	Northern Lights Aerobatic Team	**1989**	Jim Franklin
2000	John Mohr	**1988**	No winner
1999	Dan Buchanan	**1987**	The French Connection

ELAINE R. BARBER was married to the late William A. Barber. With him, she participated in air shows, met many talented pilots and became part of the aviation community. Elaine has degrees in nursing and art, an unusual combination. Currently she is a registered nurse in Howell, Michigan. Prior to this nursing position, Elaine owned and operated an art and frame gallery in Dexter, Michigan for 12 years. Elaine's inspiration for *The Adventures of Little Billy Barber* was Bill's passion for and early pursuit of flying. *Billy's First Flight Lesson* is her first children's book.

LINDA TERENTIAK is a native of Waterford, Michigan with a Bachelor of Fine Art/Commercial Art degree from Central Michigan University.

In 1985 Linda attended her first air show and fell in love with aviation. She began producing aviation artwork from photography of various aircraft that she took whenever she went to an air show. As a professional graphic artist she has been commissioned to create many pen and ink as well as watercolor works for pilots and aviation enthusiasts.

In 1989 she joined the Yankee Air Museum at Willow Run Airport, Ypsilanti, Michigan. As a Museum member Linda has been able to fly in vintage World War II military aircraft (B-17, B-25 and C-47) both in Michigan and out-of-state air shows.